On Christmas Eve

On Christmas Eve Text copyright © 1938 and 1965 by Roberta B. Rauch Illustrations copyright © 1996 by Nancy Edwards Calder   Printed in Mexico.   All rights reserved. Library
of Congress Cataloging-in-Publication Data   Brown, Margaret Wise, 1910–1952. On
Christmas Eve / by Margaret Wise Brown ; illustrated by Nancy Edwards Calder.   p.   cm.
Summary: Unable to sleep on Christmas Eve, four children creep downstairs to see the tree,
their stockings, their wrapped gifts, and to hear the singing of the carolers. ISBN 0-06-
023648-5. — ISBN 0-06-023649-3 (lib. bdg.)   [1. Christmas—Fiction.]   I. Calder, Nancy
Edwards, ill.   II. Title. PZ7.B8163On   1996 93-43636 [E]—dc20 CIP   AC
Typography by Al Cetta   ❖ Newly Illustrated Edition

On Christmas Eve

MARGARET WISE BROWN

ILLUSTRATED BY

NANCY EDWARDS CALDER

HARPERCOLLINSPUBLISHERS

*I*t was the middle of the night.
And night of all nights it was Christmas.

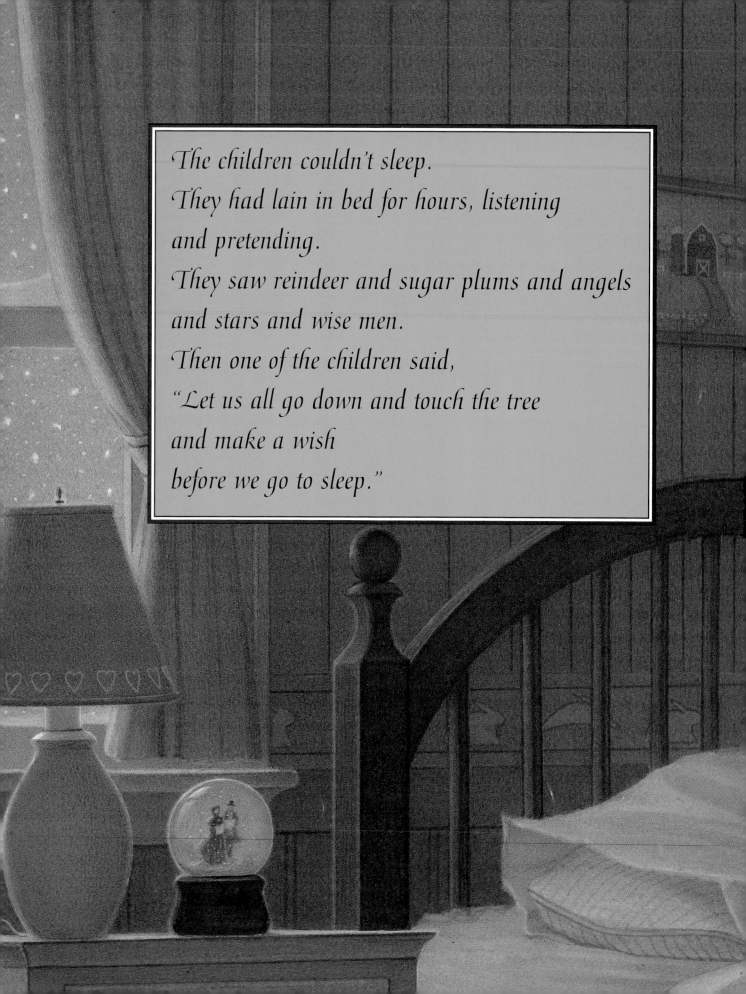

The children couldn't sleep.
They had lain in bed for hours, listening
and pretending.
They saw reindeer and sugar plums and angels
and stars and wise men.
Then one of the children said,
"Let us all go down and touch the tree
and make a wish
before we go to sleep."

So very quietly, in the large cold playroom,
they took their clothes under the covers and dressed themselves.
They put on their sweaters and slippers and socks
and bathrobes.

In the big quiet house where the people were sleeping,
the children got out of their beds.

Then into the upstairs hall they went—
quietly, almost without breathing
they went, past the door where Mother and Father were sleeping.
So quietly through the hall. No sound until the top stair creaked.

Then they all stood terribly still and listened.
No sound but their own thumping hearts.
And now they were creeping downstairs in the middle of the night—
night of all nights—Christmas night.

Out the window it even looked like Christmas.
The quietest night in the world with snow falling
so softly. So quietly.
Great green evergreen branches on the stairs
and red holly berries in the hall.

Downstairs it was still warm. The warm smells
of Christmas, pine trees and wood smoke and oh wonderful
smell of Christmas seals and packages not yet opened.
The night before Christmas, Christmas Eve.

Quietly listening, listening all over, with eyes and ears
and hands and feet they went down into the warm dark
pine-scented hall.

They came to the living room door. They listened.

Beyond the windowpane, white flakes
in the blue night, the snow fell down. They couldn't hear it.
A piece of wood creaked in the dying fire.

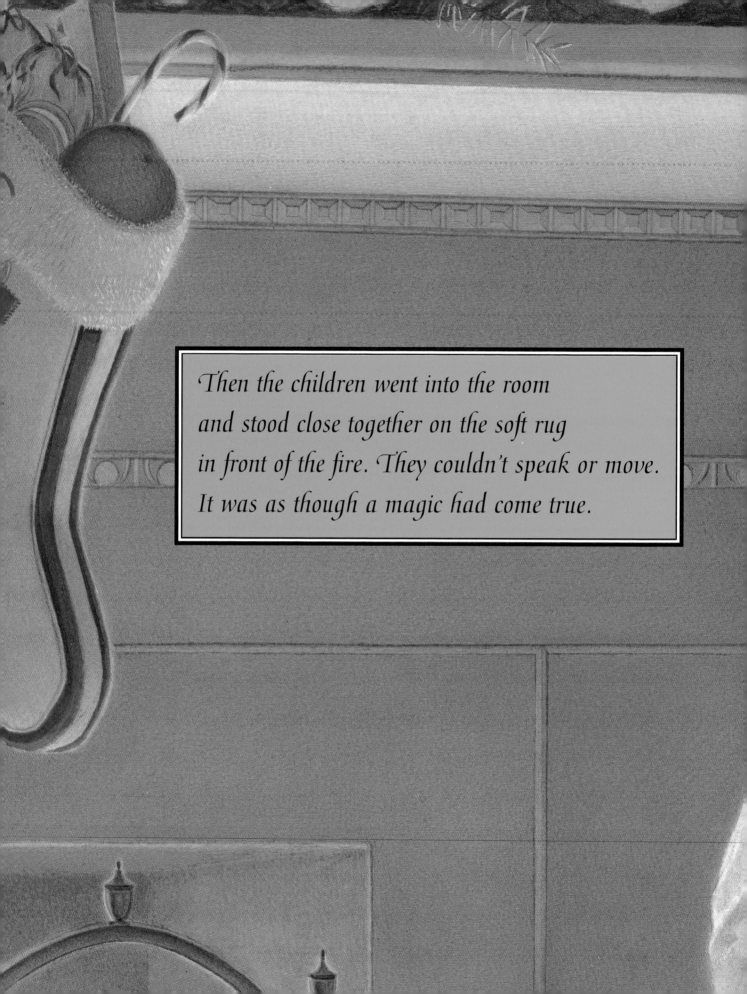

Then the children went into the room
and stood close together on the soft rug
in front of the fire. They couldn't speak or move.
It was as though a magic had come true.

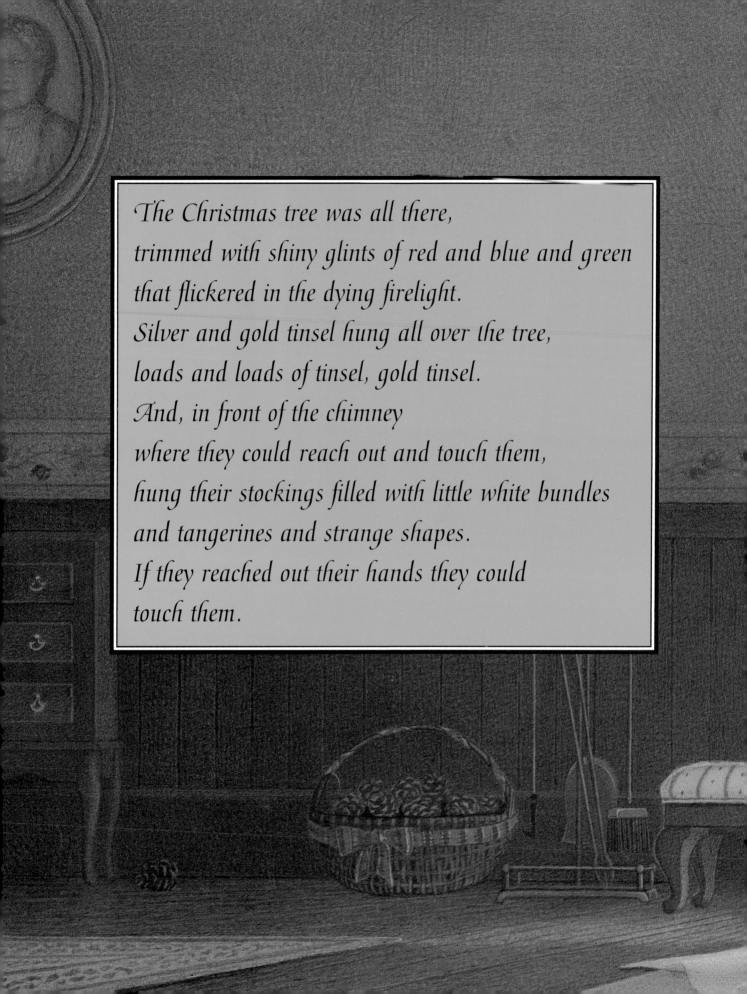

The Christmas tree was all there,
trimmed with shiny glints of red and blue and green
that flickered in the dying firelight.
Silver and gold tinsel hung all over the tree,
loads and loads of tinsel, gold tinsel.
And, in front of the chimney
where they could reach out and touch them,
hung their stockings filled with little white bundles
and tangerines and strange shapes.
If they reached out their hands they could
touch them.

Under the tree were more packages. And there was one big package. They all saw it. It looked like an electric train.

It went all around the tree.
They all saw it. No one spoke. No one moved.

And then suddenly in the night,
through the soft snow falling outside, the voices came.
They really came, those voices,
so quietly in the night singing:

"Holy Night Silent Night All is calm All is bright"
The children ran to the window.
Dark figures were moving outside in the snow.

The dark figures carried a lantern. They were
grown-up people singing. The children listened.
The sound of the voices seemed to fall with the snow.

"Sleep in heavenly peace
Sleep in heavenly peace"

The song stopped. There was that quietness
of the snow again. The grown-up people
moved around outside, dark figures
against the white snow.
The Christmas Carolers. They were
the Christmas Carolers, grown-up people who went
from house to house singing Christmas songs
on Christmas Eve.

The children quickly turned toward the stairs.
They went up the stairs almost running,
only as quietly still as they could.

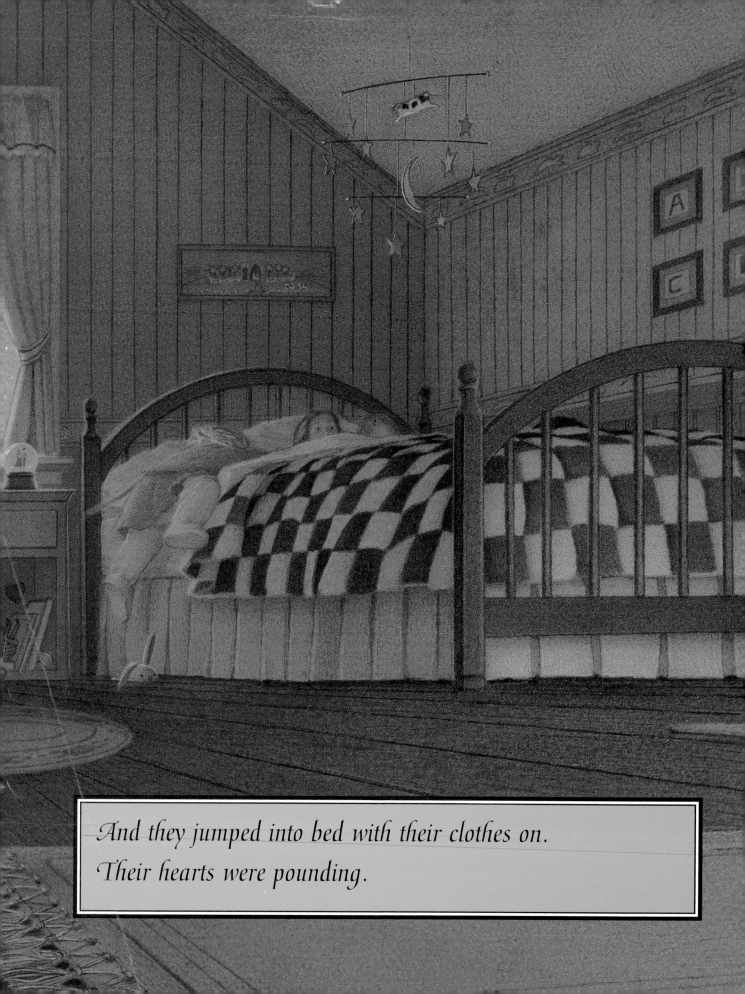

And they jumped into bed with their clothes on.
Their hearts were pounding.

Then the singing began again:
  "God rest you merry gentlemen
    Let nothing you dismay
      Oh Tidings of Comfort and Joy."